THIS BOOK BELONGS :

_____

_____

I've Only Got Three Hands !

Sigal Adler

Big problems were brewing in monster land

Where one boy's bedroom was way out of hand;

When bedtime came, well, his room was a mess!

And that mischievous monster couldn't care less.

Mrs. Monster tidied up all by herself

Straightening clothes and toys on the shelf

Making the bed and sweeping the floors

Though he had promised to do all his chores.

The boy asked, "Let's read now—all right?"

But his mother got mad: maybe later tonight

There's piles of papers and big rubber bands,

And I can't do it all with only three hands!"

She piled the toys from all over the room

And swept out the corners with a great big broom.

Now everything was finally back in its place

The laundry picked up without any trace.

When she was done, her son just whined,

"Tell me a story, I don't care what kind."

Mom said, exhausted, "A short one, that's it,

"I'll read more tomorrow, just clean up a bit."

But the next day at bedtime nothing had changed

His toys were all messy, the clothes rearranged.

The bedroom was even worse than before

But he still wanted stories, not one but more.

"There just isn't time, my sweet little boy

If you tidied up, we'd have time to enjoy

I really hoped we could read more today

But I only have three hands—what can I say?"

The next night the boy knew only too well

If he didn't clean up, there'd be no story to tell.

His Mom hadn't threatened to punish her son

He just needed sleep when his full day was done.

So that four-handed monster sighed heavily.

"Well, someone should do it – I guess that means me."

He tidied the room just as quick as a shot

Putting almost everything back in its spot.

One hand gathered books and one slid them in place,

A third picked up clothes, and a fourth scratched his face.

When Mom came and saw the orderly scene,

She smiled and said, "You made it so clean!

Now we have time for whatever you choose."

And the boy was simply thrilled at the news.

They had an amazing, wonderful night,

Lots of scary stories, packed full of fright

For monsters are slightly differently made

And love reading stories that make them afraid.

After their stories they still had more time

So the mother sang him an old bedtime rhyme

It wasn't a song we might sing with a kiss

Instead, it went just a little like this:

Goodnight my sweet, delightful boy,

I'll make you cockroach soup, what a joy!

And for dessert, I promise, don't cry,

All coated with sugar: a tasty sweet fly!

The mischievous boy thought of flies in a heap

As his eyes slowly closed and he drifted to sleep,

Tired and satisfied, and a little afraid

And all 'cause he'd tidied up after he'd played.

And since then that monster has taken great care

To keep his room tidy up here and down there.

And if you haven't cleaned up yet, you should.

So you'll have more time for things that are good.

One hand for your books, one to slide them in place,

A third for your clothes, and a fourth to scratch your face.

What's that, you say? You've only got two?

Well, boy—I sure feel sorry for you!

Good night!!!

Publish and printed in USA, 2017

Adler.sigal@gmail.com

Made in the USA
San Bernardino, CA
25 March 2020